ZOO FUN

Written by
Sarah Toast

Cover illustrated by   Interior illustrated by
Eddie Young   **Joe Veno**

Louis Weber, C.E.O.
Publications International, Ltd.
7373 North Cicero Avenue
Lincolnwood, Illinois 60646

Manufactured in U.S.A.

8 7 6 5 4 3 2 1

ISBN: 0-7853-1069-X

PUBLICATIONS INTERNATIONAL, LTD.

Little Rainbow is a trademark of Publications International, Ltd.

Mark and Mindy like being next-door neighbors. But there's something even better than being each other's neighbor: They are neighbors to the city zoo.

Mark and Mindy visit the zoo a lot. This morning, they decide to play a little game as they walk through the zoo.

"Look at the neat animals on the gate!" says Mindy, as they go through the entrance gate.

"We should try to visit all of these animals today," says Mark.

"It looks like the elephant and the giraffe are waiting for us," says Mindy. "Let's go see them first."

The huge elephant is giving a tiny bird a morning shower from its long, strong trunk. The elephant is the biggest land animal on earth, but it only eats plants.

"I'd like to have a trunk to pick up really big and heavy things," says Mark.

"I'd like to water the garden with my trunk," says Mindy.

The long-necked giraffe can be seen above the treetops. Mark and Mindy stroll over for a closer look.

The giraffe is the tall, silent type, steadily munching on the tender leaves at the tips of the topmost branches.

Mark and Mindy stretch themselves as tall as they can. They agree that they would like to be as tall as a giraffe and see for miles.

"Roar! Roar!" Mark and Mindy hear the lions' thunderous roar and run to find them. They see not one but two lions having a contest to find out which big lion can roar the loudest.

The shaggy-maned male lions roar the
most, but the female lions are the ones
that hunt for most of the lion
family's food.

Mark and Mindy pretend
to roar like big lions.

Mark and Mindy hear the chattering of seven lively monkeys and dash over to watch them. The monkeys swing between branches, holding on with their hands and feet and using their long grasping tails mostly for balance. When they want to, monkeys can move fast.

Mark and Mindy would like to have fun all day like the monkeys. Mark says, "I'd eat bananas for breakfast, lunch, and dinner."

Mindy says, "I'd never walk on the ground. I'd swing from tree to tree."

Mark and Mindy catch sight of a herd of gazelles leaping gracefully in a grassy field. The two friends bound over to watch the swift-footed gazelles speeding along.

"I'd like to run so fast I seem to fly," says Mark.

"And I'd like to leap high and far," says Mindy. "We could really go places!"

Mark and Mindy run like gazelles.

Next the two friends visit the bottle-nosed dolphins in their pool. The playful dolphins are a small type of whale. The dolphins swim fast to catch fish, but they also swim just for fun.

"If we could swim underwater, we could swim around the world through all the oceans," says Mark, as he and Mindy pretend to swim as fast as dolphins.

Penguins are birds that don't fly, but they swim very well. The penguins like to belly flop on snow and ice, then dive into the cold water. When they swim, their wings are like flippers and they steer with their webbed feet.

"I'd like to have that much fun in cold weather," says Mark.

"I'm not sure I could swim in such cold water, though," says Mindy. Mark and Mindy waddle and toddle like the penguins on the ice.

Next Mark and Mindy go inside the darkened bat house. When their eyes get used to the darkness, Mark and Mindy can see dozens of bats swooping around the room.

Bats aren't birds, but they have large wings and fly at night. By listening to echoes of their own squeaks, bats can find insects to eat.

Mark and Mindy pretend they have wings. "I'd like to swoop through the air like a bat," says Mark.

"But would you like to sleep all day and eat bugs at night?" asks Mindy.

"We did it!" says Mindy as they leave through the zoo gate. "Let's play the animal game again tomorrow."